Augustus Charles Thompson

Happy New Year

A Gift and a Greeting

Augustus Charles Thompson

Happy New Year
A Gift and a Greeting

ISBN/EAN: 9783337406967

Printed in Europe, USA, Canada, Australia, Japan

Cover: Foto ©Andreas Hilbeck / pixelio.de

More available books at **www.hansebooks.com**

HAPPY NEW YEAR:

A Gift and a Greeting.

BY A. C. THOMPSON,

AUTHOR OF "THE BETTER LAND," "THE MERCY SEAT,"
"MORAVIAN MISSIONS," ETC.

NEW YORK:
ANSON D. F. RANDOLPH & CO.
900 BROADWAY, CORNER TWENTIETH STREET.
1883.

CONTENTS.

Contents.

INTRODUCTORY.

IT is well for the world that one day at least should annually be made an epoch of good feeling. The mere expression of a kind wish helps to its own fulfillment. Our periodical congratulations are something more than mere compliments; they stir the better feelings of the heart, and the general pulse of good neighborhood is sensibly quickened. What pleasing rivalries at home! What ingenious devices for getting the precedence! The light of a smile so wide-spread lingers for days in our social firmament. Even in this age of hurry and pressure, who cannot find a moment on the first of January for the interchange of good wishes?

The custom now referred to is one of the pleasant things that link us to old times. Our Saxon forefathers made New Year's Day an occasion of festivity. The Druids, golden knife in hand, cut branches of the sacred mistletoe, and distributed them as gifts to the people. The Romans sacrificed to Janus — the patron of husbandry and peace — for whom January was named; and as they met on the street, would exchange greetings, *Annum novum faustum felicemque tibi*. Similar was it among Persians and Scandinavians. However diverse the season in various lands, when an old year ends and a new one begins, the average cheeriness of the world has immemorially risen many per cent on the first day of the first month. In Germany it is no unusual thing, especially in university towns, as the clock strikes twelve at midnight, to hear a *Vivat Neujahr* or *Prosit Neujahr* ring through the streets.

New Year's gifts have also long had their place. At Rome, for instance, the people sent presents — clients to their patrons, citizens to

---

the magistrates, and friend to friend. A book has been one of the favorite tokens of remembrance. In the Library of the British Museum there are several old publications, with titles which suggest how prevalent was the custom of making this sort of presents, though the contents might have no reference to the first day of the year: *A New Year's Gift, dedicated to the Pope's Holiness*, 1579. *A New Year's Gift, to be presented to the King's most excellent Majestie: with a petition from his loyale Subjects*, 1646. King Edward VI, having sent twenty pounds to the learned Bucer, that he might supply himself with a needed comfort, to which he had been accustomed in Germany, Bucer in return wrote a book entitled, *Concerning the Kingdom of Christ*, as a New Year's gift for his majesty. Thomas Becon, a laborious English Reformer, penned a work founded upon Isaiah IX, entitled *A New Year's Gift*. It was dedicated to a friend, and the author states: "In this, my New Year's Gift, I have opened many goodly and godly things."

When Antipater, king of Macedonia, was once presented with a book treating of happiness, he simply said, "I have no leisure." One mistake of the giver was, he did not select New Year's Day; and it certainly was a mistake to elaborate a treatise, instead of the brief and customary, "Health and happiness to the king!" But Antipater, besides being a very busy man, was a bad man, and knew nothing about happiness or the way to find it.

This little volume does not presume to rank as a treatise; it only contains a few hints on happiness. Lavater once wrote, on the first day of January, "I resolved to wish no one a Happy New Year with my lips only." To every reader there goes with this a cordial "Happy New Year" from

THE AUTHOR.

I.

To My Beloved Mother,

A HAPPY NEW YEAR!

My whole heart goes into the wish. If fervent desires could make this the happiest day of your life thus far, such a day should it be; and every day to come should be happier and happier still. Very little more of discomfort would you see.

Your dear face was the first object that I ever looked upon; your cradle songs were the first music I ever heard, and no prima donna can sing as you did, and as you now do. Your heart has been a cradle for me all along, and no other human being can have such a place in mine as you have. There are a good many whom I call acquaintances, and a few who are friends, but I can have only one mother.

A happy home is ours. What tranquil joys in the atmosphere that you create! How charming the tact with which you have restrained and moulded! It is not talk so much as character that has done it. Much as you have taught me, you have inspired me more. Your child

---

is in no way distinguished; but if there were distinction, I should know to whom to ascribe it. I often think of Sir Benjamin West's mother, who kissed him for one of his early efforts with the pencil. "And that kiss," said the artist, "made me a painter."

How watchful have you been about my companionship and my reading! A throne has been maintained at home, efficient yet lenient. Thanks for the sway! I am fully satisfied that an unrestrained child cannot be a happy child. Thanks that you have quietly but firmly insisted upon implicit obedience, and have always carried your point! Alas, that it should have cost you so much of patience! I would like to do now what Dr. William Goodell said, when it was too late, he wished to do: "O my kind mother! I often think, what would I not give to see thy gentle face once more, and, on my knees, to ask ten thousand pardons for every unkind word I ever answered thee, for every grief I unnecessarily caused thee."

Temptations to unbelief have sometimes come; yet the thought of my mother has uniformly banished them. You have done more for me than any volume of evidences. But for your example I should have gone less often to the throne of grace, as was true of John Newton, who, amidst perils, would sometimes cry, "My mother's God, the God of mercy, have mercy on me!"

My Beloved Mother.

Bishop Jewell had the name of his mother engraved on a signet; yours is engraved where it cannot be left behind when I go hence.

> " If, by the Saviour's grace made meet,
>   My God will own my life and love,
>   Methinks, when singing at his feet
>   Amid the ransomed throng above,
>   Thy name upon my glowing lips shall be,
>   And I will bless that grace for heaven and thee."

II.

To My Honored Father,

A HAPPY NEW YEAR!

YES, a thrice happy New Year's Day! All that warmest filial greeting can express, is now wrapped up in my good wishes.

The word Father kindles my deepest reverence and love. I have read that one of the Seven Wise Men of Greece used to say: "Prove yourself worthy of your parents." Would that I might be reckoned a child who is the second edition of yourself! I have come to understand what it is that governs your life; it evidently is principle. The meaning of that word I did not learn from the dictionary; your example has made it plain. Conscience is king with you, and you seem to be afraid of nothing but to do wrong. Truth is something very sacred in your eyes, and you are more anxious to be on the right side, than to have right on your side. Religion is no mere Sabbath affair; it gives character to the whole week and the whole year. I have noticed your calmness amidst opposition, and under the reproaches of some who appeared to be impatient at your integrity. I never dreamed that you were narrow, or that your firmness was unpleasantly severe. Now and then, when some one has said that you were rigid and needlessly afraid of new notions and ways, I have thought you were a great deal more valiant than those same free-and-easy neighbors. The least trace of sentimentalism or bigotry I have never seen; but I have seen a good deal of quiet heroism, and I now understand, much better than I could otherwise, the story of the lions' den, and of the burning fiery furnace. I see that nobility of character is found in places and stations far from any throne. You have remarked that it was said of the first Emperor Alexander of Russia: "His character was equivalent to a constitution," and of Sir John Lawrence, that his character alone was worth an army; and I am sure that in private life there may be found traits which are a reflex of holy men of old; they are a mighty power, and are worth more than Ophir.

You seem to me to be the happiest man I ever knew. I remember that along with many pertinent texts from the Bible, you once quoted from an old Roman writer: "No wicked man is happy"— *Nemo malus felix*. I believe it, and I believe a truly honest, conscientious, religious man is happy, if a happy person can anywhere be found. You once pointed me to what Samuel Pearce, whose Memoir was written by Andrew Fuller, said: " Were it not for an ungrateful heart, I should be the happiest man alive; and, that excepted, I neither expect nor wish to be happier in this world." You asked: Is not heaven epitomized in such a man?

More than once have I heard you repeat the reply of Agesilaus, king of Sparta, when inquired of about the way to be happy: "Do nothing that should make a man fear to die." Far distant be the day of your departure, my dear father; but if I survive you, I would like to do what one of the Herodian family did, who built a city in the midst of a beautiful plain, and named it in honor of his father — Antipatris for Antipater.

At this opening of the new year, let your grateful child join you at the joyous ringing of bells —

> " Ring out false pride in place and blood,
>   The civic slander and the spite;
>   Ring in the love of truth and right,
> Ring in the love of common good.
>
> " Ring in the valiant men and free,
>   The larger heart, the kindlier hand;
>   Ring out the darkness of the land,
> Ring in the Christ that is to be."

III.

To My Dear Sister,

A HAPPY NEW YEAR!

HAPPY as heart can be! It seems to me you do not need to make any great effort to have that true of yourself. The secret is an open one, and you have long been acting upon it; it is your life to try and make others happy. To observe the little devices, and the large ones too, in that line, the ingenious and gracious ways of effecting it has for a good while been my delight. On reading what Cowper says of Lady Hesketh, I thought at once of my dear sister: "Lady Hesketh pleases everybody, and is pleased, in her turn, with everything she finds at Olney; is always cheerful and sweet-tempered, and knows of no pleasure equal to that of communicating pleasure to us, and to all around her. This disposition in her is the more comfortable because it is not the humor of the day, a sudden flash of benevolence and good spirits occasioned merely by a change of scene, but it is her natural turn, and has governed all her conduct since I knew her first." There must be a great amount of reciprocal enjoyment, and that too of the most delicate kind. The joy of one's existence depends largely upon the number whom we love and benefit, and the number who, in turn, love us; and how many such there are in your case, it is not easy to tell. Was there any other human being of whom Frederick the Great would say as much as of Wilhelmina? "She is a sister who has all my heart and all my confidence; and whose character is of price beyond all the crowns in this universe."

Ah, what a debt do brothers owe to such women! But for them, civilized communities might be in danger of relapsing into barbarism. How great was the indebtedness of Goethe to his sister Cornelia; of Schleiermacher to his sister Charlotte; of John Aiken to his sister Lætitia, Mrs. Barbauld; of Sir William Herschel to his sister Caroline! So too of Lord Macaulay to his sisters. After the removal of the youngest of them, he says: "What she was to me no words can express. I will not say she was dearer to me than anything in the world, for my sister who was with me was equally dear; but she was as dear to me as one human being can be to another." Wordsworth confesses to a deep impression made upon him by the character of his sister Dorothy, two years younger than himself. He describes her as the blessing of his boyhood and his manhood.

My Dear Sister.

"She gave me eyes, she gave me ears,
And humble cares, and delicate fears;
A heart, the fountain of sweet tears,
And love, and thought, and joy."

You will recall the remark made by a lady of keen observation and wide experience, in regard to a friend of ours: "He must have grown up among affectionate sisters," and when inquired of: "Why do you think so?" she replied: "Because of the rich development of all the tender feelings of the heart." Samuel Adams had the amiable and valued Mary Adams in mind, when he said: "That is a happy young man who has had an elder sister upon whom he could rely for advice and counsel in youth."

I remember that it was owing to the persuasion and example of his sister Macrina, that Basil the Great, who began a professional career as a lawyer, with success, devoted himself to a religious life; and who can forget Perpetua, at her martyrdom, calling for her brother and another Christian, and saying to them: "Continue firm in the faith; love one another, and be not offended at our sufferings." What a mutual benediction were the pious Paschal, and the no less devout Jacqueline! What a beautiful religious life was that of Sir Robert Boyle and his sister, Lady Ranelagh, their affection ennobled by a forty years' community of highest interests and pursuits,

and by reciprocal helpfulness! There was scarcely
week's difference between the hours of their departu:
and they were buried, at the same time, in the chancel
St. Martins-in-the-Fields.

> " More constant than the evening star
> Which mildly beams above ;
> Than diadem — oh ! dearer far
> A sister's gentle love !

> " Gem of the heart ! Life's gift divine,
> Bequeathed us from above,
> Glad offering at affection's shrine,
> A sister's holy love ! "

IV.

To My Dear Brother,

A HAPPY NEW YEAR!

"THE congratulations of the season," sounds all too formal. What I mean is a right earnest wish, over and over, for a Happy New Year's Day.

We may well be grateful for having the same father and mother — so thoughtful, so tender, so patient were they! The same words of wisdom, the same affectionate look for both of us, the same gentle hand on the head of each! If there were no other reason, I should love you because the same blood runs in your veins as in mine.

But there is something besides parentage that moves my heart. What a companionship in sports, in plans, in aspirations! And then how much do I owe to you for being what you are! I do not think either of us answers very well to the Prodigal Son, nor to his older brother. Sure I am that neither has wanted a division of the estate, and that neither has reproached the other for riotous living. Your affection is a fortune to me. It

—19—

would be a difficult problem to determine how much happier and better, as well as better off I am, for having such a brother. Parting from the homestead became an unwelcome necessity; but what David Brainerd said, under similar circumstances, comes to mind: "I love him better than any creature living." Nor do I forget what Krummacher wrote: "Oh, how dear, how dear my brother Emil is to me! All the friends I ever lose I find in him again, and I might almost say, in a nobler form than ever."

Yes, I am largely your debtor. In many ways have you helped, and are helping me. James Beattie, the poet, was aided in his collegiate course by his brother David; Sir James Simpson by his brother Alexander; and Daniel Webster, amidst early professional studies, made strenuous efforts that he might assist his brother; but was there in either case, more of devotion by the one, or more of indebtedness, in certain respects, by the other, than is true between us?

What if we are not widely known in the world; what if our names are not to go into history — like the brothers James and Jude, Simon and Matthew, sons of Cleopas and Mary; James and John, sons of Zebedee and Salome; Peter and Andrew, sons of Jonas; Basil the Great and Gregory of Nyssa; the artists, Giovanni and Gentile

My Dear Brother.

Bellini; the men of science, William and Alexander von Humboldt; the eminent civilians, Sir Robert Grant, Governor of Bombay, and Charles Grant, Lord Glenelg — yet was there a warmer attachment between any two of them, than between us?

Can it be only some months, or is it now years and years, since we shook hands at parting? It seems like an age. What a joyful hour it was, when, after a separation of thirteen years, Columbus and his brother met on the island of Hispaniola; and when, after forty years, Moses and Aaron greeted each other in the land of Midian; and, most pathetic of all fraternal meetings — when that disclosure took place in an Egyptian palace, " I am Joseph, your brother ! "

My thoughts are also on another, the Son of the Highest, " who is not ashamed to call us brethren;" who came not only from the bosom of the Father, but also from the home of a carpenter, who presents himself as Elder Brother to the sons of toil, of want, of sorrow — a Brother to all, a Brother indeed; and whose love is the highest joy of your heart. Thanks that there is no occasion for me to say with Edith Challis, of London, England: "I am glad that I have no brothers and sisters, that I may regard Jesus Christ as my only Brother!"

— 21 —

Happy New Year

" What is the name of Christ, my Lord,
  To me the sweetest in his Word,
  Which on my heart I most record ?
    It is — ' My Brother.'

" In sacred musings oft, alone,
  My heart soars to Him on his throne,
  And sweetly feels that we are one,
    I and ' My Brother.' "

V.

To My Devoted Wife,

A HAPPY NEW YEAR!

THE earnestness of this wish cannot well be told. No one on earth knows my heart so well as you do, and I should not dare to exaggerate; nor is there any need of it. The simple truth is, if a happier man than myself can be found, I know not where to look for him; and among the human sources of my happiness you are the chief. It seems only like paying a debt, or rather paying partial interest on a debt, for me to desire that this anniversary may find you the happiest of mortals. I have never said you were something superhuman, though the word angel is often at my tongue's end; nor have I ever professed to be unutterably delighted; but this I must say, that every week there is so much of disinterestedness on your part, such absence of peevishness and fault-finding; so cheerful are looks and tones, that the domestic charm is complete. Home is the brightest spot under the sun to me. And then, I greatly admire its order, its neatness, and the statesmanlike way domestic affairs are administered. A quiet day there surpasses any attraction elsewhere. It is simply Paradise regained. Do you not remember what Franklin says about a certain cheerful man? I do; and I have not very far to go to find a counterpart. "I noticed," he says, "a mechanic among a number of others, at work on a house erected a little way from my office, who always appeared to be in a very merry humor, who had a kind word and a cheerful smile for every one he met. Let the day be ever so cold, gloomy, and sunless, a happy smile danced like a sunbeam on his cheerful countenance. Meeting him one morning, I asked him the secret of his happy flow of spirits. 'No secret, doctor,' he replied; 'I have got one of the best of wives, and when I go to work she always has a kind word of encouragement for me, and when I go home she meets me with a smile and a kiss, and she is sure to be ready; and she has done so many things, during the day, to please me, that I cannot find it in my heart to speak unkindly to anybody.'" Edmund Burke used to say that every care vanished the moment he entered his own house, and a much smaller man can say the same. If you have forgotten, I certainly have not, the tribute which Sir James McIntosh pays to his wife: "She propped my weak and irresolute nature; she urged my indolence to all the exertions that have been useful and creditable to me, and she was at hand to admonish my heedlessness or improvidence. To her I owe whatever I am; to her whatever I shall be." If you open the Memoir of Dr. William Ellis, of Madagascar memory, you will find a heavy pencilling of mine alongside the following: "For twenty years under the sweetest, strongest influence of one whose form personified all that is delicate and pure, and whose whole career was the exemplification of whatever is elevated and refined — not in external accomplishments, but in sentiment and feeling. To have been associated, as I have been, with such a being and not to have imbibed some of the transcendent excellences with which the Father of mercies so richly invested her character, was impossible." The richest gift from Heaven to me, too, is the treasure that came on our bridal day.

> " His house she enters, there to be a light,
>   Shining within, when all without is night;
>   A guardian angel o'er his life presiding,
>   Doubling his pleasures, and his cares dividing;
>   Winning him back, when mingling with the throng—
>   Back from a world we love, alas! too long—
>   To fireside happiness, to hours of ease,
>   Blest with that charm, the certainty to please.
>   How oft her eyes read his; her gentle mind
>   To all his wishes, all his thoughts inclined,
>   Still subject, ever on the watch to borrow
>   Mirth of his mirth, and sorrow of his sorrow."

VI.

To My Beloved Husband,

A HAPPY NEW YEAR!

You seem so brimful of contentment and good feeling generally, that wishes for more are almost out of place. Sunshine is never wanting when you are within doors. The sound of your step is music. Do you know I never saw a frown on your face when looking at me? — and I have often wondered it should be so. Yours is not a mechanical nor a chronic smile, but a good honest look of something besides dissatisfaction. At Roman weddings was not the gall taken out of the bird they sacrificed, that there might be no bitterness in the marriage union? As for grumbling — at any rate about the family and its affairs — you seem to reckon that among the lost arts. You have acted on John Wesley's saying, "I dare no more fret than curse or swear."

I notice that at the table you never speak of losses or injuries, of deaths or funerals. And then you are always looking on the bright side of things, and the bright side of character — not croaking nor carping, and so making yourself and the rest of us miserable. You once said, before we were married, that you hoped we should be able to get on with borrowing very little, and least of all, borrowing trouble; and afterwards, you said that, as a general thing, troubles which never come do the most mischief. I have learned to agree with you.

True we have been down into the valley of Bochim together; but, for the most part, our Heavenly Father has led us into green pastures. When trial or danger has come, I have never questioned the sincerity or promptness of your sympathy. In the way of contrast I have now and then thought of Budæus, the learned librarian to Francis I. His servant, as you well remember, came running to him one day in a great fright, to say that the house was on fire. Hardly raising his eyes from the book before him: "Go," said he, "and inform your mistress. It is her concern. You know I never interfere in domestic matters." I can forgive David Hume for some of the naughty words he wrote, because of his writing this, that for a man to be born with a fixed disposition always to look at the bright side of things, is a far happier.thing than to be born to a fortune of ten thousand a year. This habit of yours has helped to keep the wedding ring bright, and has kept me reminded of the old saying: "As your wedding ring wears, your cares will wear away."

I verily believe that our match was made in heaven;

and though I never thought we were a couple of angels, I do sometimes call to mind what an old German historian says about Louis and Elizabeth of Hungary : " They loved each other with a love that was both human and divine; and angels came down and dwelt with them."

I am satisfied that no true happiness comes except as the gift and blessing of God. There is another word, sounding a good deal like happiness, and which must always go with it, and that is holiness. But for the love of God shed abroad in the heart, and but for an abiding trust in Him, I am sure you could not be what you are to the family.

> " A man he seems of cheerful yesterdays
> And confident tomorrows ; with a face
> Not worldly-minded, for it bears too much
> Of Nature's impress — gayety and health,
> Freedom and hope ; but keen, withal, and shrewd.
> His gestures note — and hark ! his tones of voice
> Are all vivacious as his mien and looks."

VII.

To My Dear Daughter,

A HAPPY NEW YEAR!

MANY, many happy returns of the day; and may every returning New Year be brighter than the one before it! My ardent prayer for you, precious daughter, is that you may have the one thing needful — that which can make every day a joy; which will be no less fresh when December thirty-first comes round; and which will stay by in every situation of life. You know what it is — the Pearl of great price, the treasure and ornament that serve good purpose as nothing else can, in hours of loneliness, disappointment and suffering. It keeps one from being moody and despondent. It gilds everything otherwise dark. It makes life seem noble. It sweetly harmonizes the present and the future. You do well to apprehend this, that God did not make us in order that we might be happy at all events, do or be what we may. We can achieve the highest good in only one way, the way which he has appointed.

I often think of an incident mentioned by Rev. Eustace

Carey, the missionary, who, in visiting a young native
convert one day, asked her how she felt. Her reply was:
"Happy! happy! I have Christ here," laying her hand
on the Bible, "and Christ here," pressing it to her
heart, " and Christ there," pointing towards heaven.
A girl to be envied surely, whatever her color, culture,
or surroundings. Was she not rich beyond any Eastern
nabob? Such wealth may indeed be obtained on earth,
but not from earth. Flesh and blood cannot reveal it;
it is a boon from above, and yet may be had by any one,
and may be had for the asking.

I must remind you of Madame de Staël, the most
brilliant woman and the most eminent female writer of
her period, who complained that the only one of her
powers which had been fully developed was the faculty
of suffering, and who, with all her genius and culture,
was, to an unusual degree, unhappy. Her work, *Dix
Années d'Exil*, is one of the most painful you will ever
read. Her first marriage added nothing to her comfort;
her second marriage detracted from her reputation. And
this reminds me to caution you on the subject of ambitious
marriages. You will find that when position has large
influence in such matters, the proportion of happy unions
is very small; and not less true will you find this when
wealth, real, or supposed, is the determining motive. The
wider your acquaintance with the world becomes, the

more frequently will you be reminded of Queen Zenobia, taken to Rome, a captive in golden chains.

I have never distrusted your heart, my dear child; I pray the Saviour may have no occasion to distrust it either. Be assured, no flowery path promises so much as does the path to the cross. Kneel there in penitent confession of sinfulness, in a sense of helplessness, looking with faith to the atoning Saviour, and let all your faculties, powers and acquisitions be stamped with his precious name. Then will you be enriched to all eternity with a share in the Unspeakable Gift, and happy indeed will be every New Year's Day. Lady Margaret, a sister of Lady Huntingdon, once said to her, and said truthfully: "Since I have known and believed in the Lord Jesus Christ, I have been as happy as an angel."

> "Whilst I feel Thy love to me,
>   Every object teems with joy;
> Here, O may I walk with Thee,
>   Then into Thy presence die!
> Let me but Thyself possess,
>   Total sum of happiness!
> Real bliss I then shall prove,
>   Heaven below, and heaven above."

VIII.

To My Dear Son,

A HAPPY NEW YEAR!

HOW earnest the wish is cannot well be told. God grant that this morning of the year may be all bright and beautiful with the light of his countenance! No other sunshine reaches the soul.

About gifts I will say nothing except that if all lands with their products were mine to bestow, they would be nothing to what I have in mind as your portion — the greatest possible gift, and what can come only from heaven. Happiness as a direct object of pursuit is never overtaken. The great Fountain of holiness and of all that is good and excellent must be sought, and found, and loved with the whole heart. In giving himself God enriches boundlessly; and he offers to do it freely. If, without that, he were to make over to you everything else, it would not make you happy. The soul was designed to be completely suited and satisfied with nothing less than the Holy One, the God of infinite love.

Genius, whether speculative, imaginative, or whatever

its type, is altogether insufficient. The philosopher Kant found less to cheer him in this first month of the year than in the second, because that is the shortest, and not long before the close of life, he wrote: "O happy February! in which man has least to bear — least pain, least sorrow, least self-reproach." Listen to another German: "I hate the world! I hate myself! No one cares for me! I have genius; yet I am treated like a Pariah! I have a heart; yet I have no one to love! I am completely miserable!" Thus did the celebrated composer, Beethoven, vent his wretchedness to a fellow musician, as they paced the streets of his native city, one night. Molière, the prince of French comic writers, made his house gloomy with sadness; and while Cervantes made all Spain laugh at his humorous sallies, he was himself the victim of deep melancholy. Byron, in spite of poetic eminence, and the auxiliaries of rank and fortune, sighed with the prodigal's sigh:

> "The fire that on my bosom preys,
> Is lone as some volcanic isle;
> No torch is lighted at its blaze,
> A funeral pile!"

What man is fit to be left to himself, or being so left, will fail of being wretched? Nothing is so great an evil as that which separates from God; everything that draws to Him is a benediction.

My Dear Son.

You have no reason, and I trust no disposition, to doubt this. Experience, whether of those younger or older, confirms it. "The Lord is the portion of mine inheritance," was the testimony of one, three thousand years ago. Two hundred years ago, the able and learned John Howe, finding there was nothing lower on which his soul could rest — for nothing lower is itself at rest — made this deliberate declaration: "Lo! I come to Thee — the Eternal Being, the Spring of Life, the Centre of Rest, the Stay of the Creation, the Fullness of all things. I join myself to Thee; with Thee I will lead my life and spend my days, with whom I aim to dwell forever, expecting when my little time is over, to be taken up ere long into thy eternity." One hundred years ago, David Brainerd could say: "O, one hour with God infinitely exceeds all the pleasures and delights of this lower world." And no wonder; God is greater than his gifts; he himself is more than the sum of them. He is the comprehensive good, the universal good. If your heart goes forth in the utterance, "My God," you are made forever; you belong to the side that cannot fail to win; you may "drink of the river of his pleasures" — the river that went out of Eden, and that still waters Paradise. I have known such; my strongest wish for you, my dear son, is that you may be one of them.

Happy New Year!

"Always his downcast eye
Was laughing silently,
As if he found some jubilee in thinking;
For his one thought was God,
In that one thought he abode,
Forever in that thought more deeply sinking."

—38—

IX.

To My Aged Grandmother,

A Happy New Year!

A REAL happy New Year's Day is what I wish you. Perhaps you could not be any happier than you are. You always seem to be in good spirits; and you are so kind, and have so many wise things to say, that I am in a hurry to be old and like you. The Rev. Dr. Tyng, of New York, in a lecture on aged women, said: "I would not give up the worth of my children's grandmother in my house for the best and handsomest young woman in the land." You, my dear grandmother, are not one of those fine ladies who dress young, and are always making a great effort to look and to act young. Do you think anybody respects them? Is it not a piece of vanity, with a touch of hypocrisy? Surely, the spiritual may gain more than the physical loses; and beauty of soul may keep improving faster than the hair turns white.

> " Madame, new years may well expect to find
> Welcome from you, to whom they are so kind;
> Still, as they pass, they court and smile on you,
> And make your beauty, as themselves, seem new."

In all the books of the Bible, the age of only one woman is given. Just how old you are, I do not know, and do not care to know, so you live for years to come, and grow happier all the while. Madame Rothschild, mother of the famous bankers, a bright old lady, said to the physician when she was very sick, at ninety-eight: "Dear doctor, try to do something for me." "Madame," said he, "what can I do for you? I cannot make you young again." "No, doctor, I don't want to be young again, but I want to continue to grow old." That is what I want for you.

I am sure it is not true that children are generally spoiled by their grandparents. Did not Madame Campan say, that of all the young girls committed to her care, the very best was one who had been brought up by her grandmother? Did not that excellent woman, Baroness Von Gersdorf, have charge from his childhood of her grandson, Count Zinzendorf, who became so eminent for piety and usefulness? I owe a great deal to you — more than is possible for me to repay. Your kind words and your valued maxims have sunk into my heart. And then, you never seem to be thinking about yourself; and though you are sometimes a sort of up-stairs prisoner, you keep in mind the poor and suffering, whom perhaps you have never seen, and you often send me with proofs of your remembrance. It is the best school I was ever in. I

know of one woman, besides Josephine, who might say at
the end of life, "I never caused a tear to flow." You are
a great deal stronger than if you were one of the strong-
minded. There is not a particle of the unwomanly
woman about you.

Did you ever think why the first two announcements
of our Saviour's resurrection, the first two visions of
angels and the first two appearances of Christ after his
resurrection, were made to women? One might suppose
that it would rather have been to the intimate disciples,
Peter, James and John. It must have been because those
holy women showed a peculiar tenderness and strength
of affection and loyalty. Did not Martin Luther say
rightly: "There is nothing on earth sweeter than the
heart of a woman in which piety dwells?"

At Fliedner's establishment in Kaiserswerth, Prussia,
after passing through a beautiful garden, you come to
what is named the *Feierabend Haus*, a symbolic name,
denoting "House of Rest" for the aged deaconesses.
Feierabend means the evening before a great festival.
Your house and your rooms seem just such a place.

> "Swift through the pearl-white portal
>   Thy feet may enter in —
> Into the realm of music
>   Where not a note will jar;

Happy New Year!

Into the clime of sweetness
  Which not a breath will mar;
When sighs are all out of hearing,
  And tears are all out of sight,
And the shadows of earth are forgotten,
  In the heaven which has no night."

X.

To My Revered Grandfather,

A HAPPY NEW YEAR!

HAPPY, happy — as many times as you are years old!
"At evening time there shall be light" — and light there
is, an abundance of it. I always find cheerfulness on
your face and in your voice; and when I hear old age
spoken of I never associate the idea of gloom with it.
You seem to be on a stepping-stone near heaven. Did
you ever feel melancholy? If so, was it not a great
while ago?

Solomon says: "A merry heart maketh a cheerful
countenance;" and you have told me more than once
what it is that makes your heart so glad. You have said
that every book in the Bible smells of myrrh; that the
great truths thereof fill your soul with delight; that the
divine promises bring joy unspeakable. I have noticed
your face never so shines as when you are reading the
holy volume. With such a treasure in hand — you
sometimes exclaim — who would not be buoyant? Who
that has seen, like Simeon, "the salvation prepared

before the face of all people," can be otherwise than gladsome, or do anything but look on the bright side of things!

Alas, for skeptics like Gibbon! He winds up his *Autobiography*, "I must reluctantly observe that two causes, the abbreviation of time, and the failure of hope, will always tinge with a browner shade the evening of life." After an almost unexampled career of literary eminence, caressed by prince and people, Goethe declares: "I may truly say that in seventy-five years I have not had four weeks of true comfort." The great historian and the German genius were both blind to the radiance of that kingdom which inspires a hope full of glory; they brought no frankincense to Bethlehem.

You once copied out for me the following, which I keep among my choice papers: William Romaine, when no longer young, wrote: "I have good news to tell you from a far country, as refreshing as cold water to a thirsty soul. God spared me to read over my Bible once more. O what a treasure — what unsearchable riches are there in this golden mine!" Count Oxenstiern, the well-known Swedish chancellor, in advanced years, said to Whitelock, the English ambassador: "I have seen much and enjoyed much of this world, but I never knew how to live till now. I thank my God who has given me time to know him, and likewise myself. All the comfort I have, and all the comfort I take — and which is more than the whole world can give — is the knowledge of God's love in my heart, and the reading in this blessed book," laying his hand on the Bible.

I have observed that in perusing the sacred page, there is usually an expression on your face as if you had found something peculiarly delightful, or as if you had got hold of a new and most valuable volume. It must be the warmth therefrom that keeps all frost out of your heart; for it never seems to be winter with you, but always early and golden autumn. "They shall still bring forth fruit in old age." I am reminded of what Mr. Longfellow said: "To those who ask how I can write so many things that sound as if I were a boy, please say that there is in this neighborhood, or neighboring town, a pear tree, planted by Governor Endicott, two hundred years old, and that it still bears fruit not to be distinguished from the young tree in flavor. I suppose the tree makes new wood every year, so that some part of it is always young. Perhaps that is the way with some men when they grow old; I hope it is so with me."

I am sure that "Multitude of years teach wisdom;" everybody sees on your

"Reverend head
The milk-white pledge of wisdom sweetly spread."

Happy New Year!

"The aged Christian stands upon the shore
Of Time, a storehouse of experience,
Filled with the treasures of rich heavenly lore;
I love to sit and draw from him, from thence,
Sweet recollections of his journey past,
A journey crowned with blessings to the last."

XI.

To My Dear Granddaughter,

A HAPPY NEW YEAR!

WERE you looking for a New Year's present? Would you like one of the three thousand dresses in Queen Elizabeth's wardrobe, which were chiefly an accumulation of such gifts? Perhaps not; but a token of love is just what I have in mind — something that will not wear out nor tarnish; something that shall grow brighter and more precious till the last year of life. In order to that, it must of course become a part of yourself, laid up where neither moth nor rust doth corrupt.

Miss Henrietta Neale, an English woman, on the first day of January, made this record: "Oh, that I may be enabled to seek and dig in the mines of heavenly wisdom, for that which is more precious than gold!" Lady Glenorchy, a Scottish woman, gives utterance to her feelings on a New Year's day: "O that I had a heart and tongue to praise him, and power to show to others the grace of God by a holy and useful walk and conversation! May I this year increase in faith, love and power, in my soul, that God may be glorified in me and by me." Religious character and religion in life should be foremost. A good many Christian people do not seem to be very happy, yet it is not piety, but the want of it, that makes them unhappy — the want, at least, of some element which might secure harmony and vigor, and so yield great joy.

I am not, however, going into a homily on spiritual culture. Your blessed Bible is the only treatise needed. One or two things I will suggest in the line of *petite morale*. Let it be a matter of conscience and of uniform practice to show little favors. Form the habit, and it will become a second nature, and will be the source of untold help and happiness to others, and reflexively to yourself too. There is a world of enjoyment in thus being a friend, and finding a friend. I like now and then, to repeat:

"A small unkindness is a great offence;"

"Evil is wrought
By want of thought,
As well as by want of heart."

Another thing — avoid revelling in unfounded expectations, and ideal joys. Unfading crowns are not made of fading flowers. On the other hand, my child, let it never be easy to find dark hours; and waste no time in worrying over what can be cured, or what cannot be cured. Resolve to be religiously cheerful year in and year out. Minister, as you go along, to the well-being and comfort of somebody every day. Master the beautiful art of doing this in the most delicate and unostentatious way. You were not born before the fall; and in common with the rest of the race, there is in you a streak of self-seeking, that will need to be watched narrowly. Fight against it, and fill up life with as many kind little acts as may be, done in the sweetest manner possible. That is simply Christian politeness — such as reigns in Paradise. "O divine love!" exclaims Ralph Cudworth, "the sweet harmony of souls! the music of angels! the joy of God's own heart! the very darling of his bosom! the source of true happiness! the pure quintessence of heaven! that which reconciles the jarring principles of the world, and makes them all chime together! that which melts men's hearts into one another!"

> " Love the Lord, and thou shalt see Him,
>   Do his will and thou shalt know
> How the Spirit lights the letter,
>   How a little child may go
> Where the wise and prudent stumble ;
>   How a heavenly glory shines
> In His acts of love and mercy,
>   From the Gospel's simplest lines."

XII.

To My Dear Grandson,

A HAPPY NEW YEAR!

A GREY head and a warm heart can keep company, my lad. Certainly, my wishes for you today are far from being cold ones. You may not have thought out carefully just what is meant by being happy, or what is needful in order to it. This is no time for definitions; but would you not like to have your older friend make a suggestion? I have an eye upon your future years, and should like to contribute something to the happiness of your whole life.

I suppose there are very few youths or young men, whatever their aim relative to occupation or position in life, who do not look upon riches as almost indispensable to high enjoyment. A fine thing it is, indeed, to have ample means; but I must caution you against setting the heart on wealth. The difficulty of acquiring it honestly, and of keeping it, is notorious. Do not then build upon uncertainty. If by inheritance, or in business, you become successful, beware. I wish to put great emphasis on that word, Beware. Beware of becoming a devotee to acquisition ; of being absorbed in the one thought of more money — more, more, more !

Look around. There is a man who began moderately, and was master of himself ; but the desire of gain became gradually a passion ; it has made him a bond-servant. No one in his employ is so thoroughly a drudge as he. He has sold himself to a hard task-master, and in the bargain he reserved no leisure for mental improvement, or home enjoyments, or anything but just to add to his pile of wealth. And what is he for society ; what is he for the world now ; and what is he likely to be in the world to come ?

> " Harpax, the merchant, died ; his body was dissected;
> No symptom of disease was anywhere detected,
> Until they reached the heart — which to find they were not able ;
> But in its place they found — the multiplication table."

There is no hallucination at which the Prince of Darkness grins a more ghastly smile than the mistaken idea that merely having a great deal will make one happy. During the later years of his life, the famous London banker, Nathan Rothschild, was reported to be always in fear of assassination. " You must be a very happy man," said a guest at one of the banquets for which his house in Piccadilly was famous. "Happy !

Me happy!" he exclaimed: "What, happy! when just as you are going to dine, you have a letter placed in your hands, saying: 'If you do not send me £500 I will blow your brains out!' Me happy!"

Wealth often creates more fears and more wants than it relieves. Girard, of Philadelphia, after acquiring a vast property, though supposed by some to be getting immense delight out of accumulation, wrote to a friend: "As to myself, I live like a galley-slave, constantly occupied; and often passing the night without sleeping, I am wrapped in a labyrinth of affairs, and worn out with care. I do not value fortune. The love of labor is my highest emotion. When I rise in the morning, my only effort is to labor so hard during the day, that when night comes, I may be enabled to sleep soundly."

"Upon this I awaked, and beheld," says one of the old prophets; "and my sleep was sweet unto me;" but he had no earthly possession. After all, poverty itself has some perquisites; it need not feel anxious about the stock market; it is burglar-proof. How often is it found in the very best company; and not unfrequently associated with the most honored and the most honorable! Aristides, perhaps the worthiest man of his day in all Greece, did not leave enough to pay his funeral expenses, and the same was very nearly if not quite true of William Pitt. Socrates had so little as to occasion the remark:

"Poverty has become an inmate with philosophy." Erasmus said that he desired wealth no more than a feeble beast desires a heavy burden; and Samuel Johnson declared: "Money and time are the heaviest burthens of life, and the unhappiest of all mortals are those who have more of either than they know what to do with." He and three other men of eminent talent in the last century, Collins, Fielding and Thomson, knew what it is to be arrested for debt. What makes a man poor? Not want of wealth, but want of peace, want of grace. We do not predicate poverty of the contented man. An Arabian proverb says: "Poverty, without debt, is independence." A wise Oriental writes: "There is that maketh himself rich, yet hath nothing;" and another Oriental, no less wise, writes: "I have learned, in whatsoever state I am, therewith to be content."

Ah, my grandson, settle it among your deepest purposes and convictions — settle it once for all and forever — that whatever you may possess, you will not be possessed by it; that you will never carry a hand withered by lack of giving; that you will rather be rich by laying out than by laying up; that no kind of goods deserve that name, if you do not propose to do good with them; that when you go hence, the chief question will be, not How much did he leave? but, How much did he carry with him? I commend to your careful recollection the following private entries made by the late Amos Lawrence, of Boston: "Jan. 1, 1849.—I adopted the practice ten years ago, of spending my income. My outgoes since the first of January, 1842, have been upwards of $400,000, and my property, on the first of this year, is as great as on January 1, 1842. The more I give, the more I have." "Jan. 1, 1852.—The outgoes for all objects since January 1, 1842 (ten years), have been $604,000, more than five-sixths of which have been applied in making other people happy."

A gentleman, taking a friend to the top of his house, showed him his estate. "There," said he, "do you see that farm? Well, that is mine." Then, pointing in another direction, "Do you see that house? That also belongs to me." The friend asked in turn, "Do you see that little village yonder? Well, there lives a poor woman in that village who can say more than all this?" "Ah! what can she say?" "Why, she can say, 'Christ is mine!'" To be united by faith to him, and to be like him, is to be rich now, and to be heir to the "inheritance, incorruptible, undefiled, and that fadeth not away."

> — "And said to Harry: 'In this book
> 'Tis written plain and sure,
> That what we do, not what we have,
> Will make us rich or poor.

Happy New Year!

There's not a rich man ever reached
 Heaven's high and pure abode,
There's not a rich man entering now
 The straight and narrow road,
Unless he makes, has made his wealth
 A staff, and not a load —
A staff for others. Mark you well
 The good Samaritan —
How rich he grew by what he gave
 The helpless, wounded man.' "

XIII.

To My Dear Niece,

A HAPPY NEW YEAR!

You are one of my great joys, and a great many good wishes are contained in this one of a Happy New Year! It is no small satisfaction to me that you would not care to have any article of jewelry as a gift today. The way I have heard you speak of some who are loaded down with ornaments, and decked out in finery, has led me to rank your taste and judgment high. You once said that it provoked you to see how people are estimated by what they wear rather than by what they are. I have good reason for thinking that you aspire to be a noble woman, instead of a fine lady. May you never be entrapped into the slavery of fashion — into a delirium about costly and showy furniture, decorated French porcelain, expensive candelabra, and all that sort of things. Real elegance and symmetrical arrangement are never ostentatious. Display and comfort do not keep house together. Mark it, whenever ambition to shine in dress, domestic appointments or equipage, comes in, contentment goes out.

The same may be said about the mere devotees of society. You will find a good many of them who have to apologize for their bondage and their misery; but real happiness is never trained in that school. Lady Marlborough, though her husband was at the acme of fame, and the envy of thousands, could only write: "I have no comfort in my own family, and when alone my reflections almost kill me, so that I am forced to fly to the society of those whom I detest and abhor. Now, there is Lady Frances Sanderson's great rout tomorrow night; all the world will be there, and I must go. I do hate that woman as much as I hate a physician; but I must go, if for no other purpose but to mortify and spite her."

It is an old truism that one may be eminent in rank, in talent, in art, and yet, as a woman be low, and be as wretched as she is low. Look at Madame Rachel, asking to have all her jewels brought to her bed, that she might try and get comfort out of the recollections of her triumphs as Queen of Tragedy, triumphs marked by souvenirs from most of the crowned heads of Europe; and after a glance at them, exclaiming: "Why have I to part with all this so soon!" — and then expiring. Madame de Maintenon writes to a friend: "Why can I not make you sensible of that uneasiness which preys upon the great, and the difficulty they labor under to employ their time? Do you not see that I am dying with melancholy, at a height of fortune which my imagination could once have scarcely conceived? I have been young and beautiful; have had a high relish of pleasure, and have been the universal object of love. In a more advanced age, I have spent years in intellectual pleasures; I have at last risen to favors; but I protest to you, that every one of these conditions leaves in my mind a dismal vacuity!"

It was a girl of only seven years who once said: "Mother, I have learned how to be happy, and I shall always be happy." "My dear," said her mother, "how did you learn this?" She replied: "Not to care anything about myself, but try to make every body else happy." What discovery, or what accomplishment is there superior to that? It is such whom one of the early Fathers calls "Lilies of Christ." They have his spirit; like him they go about doing good; they conquer selfishness; they do not wear out themselves or others, by worrying. If they are not angels, they are ministering spirits; by their amiability and useful industry, they create a vast amount of social sunshine. And are there any happier souls than theirs? Whatever embarrassments of natural temperament they may labor under, they are the cheery ones. "I am melancholy by nature," said Mrs. Jewsbury, "but cheerful on principle."

Happy New Year!

"I saw her upon nearer view
A spirit, yet a woman too!
Her household motions light and free,
And steps of virgin liberty;
A countenance in which did meet
Sweet records—promises as sweet;
A creature, not too bright nor good
For human nature's daily food.
A perfect woman nobly planned,
To warn, to comfort, and command,
And yet a spirit still, and bright,
With something of an angel   light."

XIV.

To My Young Nephew,

A HAPPY NEW YEAR!

GREAT happiness is my wish for you. "How shall I get it?" you ask. Well, I have a word or two about that. Real enjoyment is not only inner, but from within. Surroundings cannot create it; and it may exist in spite of any surroundings. Aristotle would make out that happiness lies in soundness and general perfection of body and mind, with a concurrence of all outward circumstances requisite. Yes, but where is the fortunate youth in whose case such a concurrence is found? or, suppose he is known to history, did he, after all, claim to be happy? "Frequently," says Rousseau, "when in possession of everything that could make life pleasing, I have been the most miserable of mortals." Means and occasions are unavailing unless the capacity is there. You might once have heard a climbing boy at work amidst the soot of a chimney, singing:

> "The sorrows of the mind
> Be banished from this place;

Religion never was designed
To make our pleasures less."

You notice that in Matthew, fifth, every benediction
is upon a quality of character, not upon outward condition; and so throughout the holy volume. Ritualism
pronounces blessings on candles, bells, beads, and what
not; but in spiritual worship devout requests are offered
in behalf of persons rather than things.

The old stoics — and modern stoics, too — have been
at fault, in proudly dreaming that happiness must not
only be in themselves, but of themselves. Schiller says:
"All my enjoyments I must dig out of my own soul."
In some sense that may of course be true; but digging
and dredging, in mere native depths, and with mere natural machinery, fail to bring pearls to the surface. "The
wicked are like the troubled sea, when it cannot rest,
whose waters cast up mire and dirt." Something from
on high is needed. The Delectable Mountains have
their heads above the clouds. "What makes you so
happy, my dear," said a relative to the lad, Rolls Plumbe,
in his sickness; and he replied with earnestness: "The
love of God! God fills my heart with his love." Another
suffering lad, James Laing, whose Memoir was written
by Robert McCheyne, said to his sister on the last day
of the year: "I will tell you what I would like for my
New Year's gift; I would like a praying heart, and a

heart to love Christ more." His desire was gratified; within twenty-four hours he could say, "This is the happiest New Year's Day that I have ever had, for I have Christ."

> " There are in this loud, stunning tide
>   Of human crime and care,
>   With whom the melodies abide
>   Of the everlasting clime,
>   Who carry music in their heart
>   Through dusky lane and wrangling mart,
>   Plying their daily task with busier feet
>   Because their secret souls a holier strain repeat.

XV.

To My Dear Friend,

A HAPPY NEW YEAR!

WITH a most sincere wish, a wish that will not fade out as the day declines, a wish rising into a prayer that this first morning of the year may be without a cloud in your inner firmament, and be the harbinger of more than three hundred and sixty-five days of serene enjoyment!

The Jews look upon New Year's Day as the anniversary of our first parents' creation. Thanks that man is; and that in the onward flow of the race, there is such an one as yourself; that, in God's good providence, your life is a benediction to many, and to myself among them! Acquaintances are numerous; friends less so, though one cannot help commiserating the man, who had been much in society, and who said his acquaintances would fill a cathedral, but a pulpit would hold all his friends. Differences in position, possessions, capacity, and temperament, do not lessen the value or the sacredness of this regard. Among the apostles, Peter and John were exceedingly unlike, and yet were warm friends; just as chemical combination takes place most readily between bodies that least resemble one another.

Every New Year's Day I have an unseen, rich gift, as I take an inventory of possessions, and feel a renewed assurance of your affection. My happiness keeps along, year in and year out. Not a little inspiration have I received from you. I think of the motto of Albert II, King of Hungary and Emperor of Germany: "A friend is the choicest treasure of life"—*Amicus optima vitæ possessio.* With the one to whom this is sent in mind, I would repeat what Goethe said: "Of all rare gifts, the rarest is the gift to be a friend."

My wishes for your welfare, and my expectations in regard to the continuance of attachment, are by no means restricted to the twelvemonth now opening, nor to any limited number of years. Looking forward, far forward, I call to mind words of the beautiful Clementine Cuvier, daughter of the celebrated naturalist: "You know you are my sister in Christ for eternity; there is nothing else deserves the name."

> " Mysterious are His ways, whose power
> Brings forth that unexpected hour,
> When minds that never met before,
> Shall meet, unite, and part no more!
> It is the allotment of the skies,

My Dear Friend.

The hand of the Supremely Wise,
That guides and governs our affections,
And plans and orders our connections,
Directs us in our distant road,
And marks the bounds of our abode."

XVI.

To My Young Friend,

A HAPPY NEW YEAR!

RIGHT hearty is the wish, and your generous disposition responds with an overflow of acknowledgments. It is a real delight to see you so buoyant.

You will not object — will you? — to a hint from your older friend. Well, be joyous, but not hilarious. Laugh, to be sure, when you must, but not with a roar. Men or boys, women or girls, who are truly happy, make no great noise about it. Napoleon Bonaparte, in his bitter chagrin at Elba, ostentatiously adopted the motto: "Happy everywhere," *Ubicumque Felix*, but nobody believed him; and as little did he believe it himself. Be honest; be natural. It is a great deal more laborious to seem happy, than to be happy.

The boisterous person is generally very vain, or perhaps somewhat intoxicated, but always very disagreeable. To be sprightly is not the same as being tumultuous. Enjoyment, if the genuine article, is sure to be characterized by a certain sobriety and self-possession, instead of being possessed by the demon of uproar. One of the sure marks of ill-breeding and want of true culture, is an unrestrained ebullition of animal spirits.

From the nature of the case, high raised joys, even though noble in their nature, cannot be lasting. It was so with Archimedes, when he leaped and shouted: "I have found it;" and so with Benjamin Franklin at the moment of his great discovery. Reaction and a degree of exhaustion are unavoidable. "O victory, victory," exclaimed Lord Nelson, "how you distress my poor head!"

Never yield then, my young friend, to turbulence of emotion. Never suffer yourself to become the victim of even pleasurable experiences. Be self-contained, and you will live to see all the more Happy New Years, besides being all the happier right along. This may not now seem to you of any great moment; but act on the suggestion, and you will by and by discover that it was worth many other gifts of the season.

> " Thus shall you find
> He most of all doth bathe in bliss,
> Who hath a quiet mind."

I love to think of the excellent Lady Huntingdon, as she came from her chamber one morning — an unwonted light on her placid countenance— and as she remarked,

with calmness: "The Lord hath been present with my
spirit this morning in a remarkable manner;" " My soul
is filled with glory; I am as in the element of heaven
itself." If anybody is to be envied, it is such an one;
and such an one as Richard Crashaw sings of — whatever
the surroundings —

> " A happy soul, that all the way
> To heaven, hath a summer's day."

XVII.

To My Aged Friend,

A HAPPY NEW YEAR!

JOY to you today! Your prolonged life is a joy to many. The Jews have this traditional saying: "An old man in a house is a good sign in it;" also, "An old woman in a house is a treasure in it." Hearty congratulations to your home, for its auspices, and for what it contains! Old furniture is now coming more and more into esteem.

What a fearful announcement it was to Eli: "There shall not be an old man in thy house forever." We love to ponder on that Bible phrase: "In a good old age;" and on another phrase: "They shall bring forth fruit in old age." That is what the Stuyvesant pear tree is doing, and what you are doing. You seem to have entered into covenant with youth, a good while ago, never to part company; and hence your heart has been kept from growing old. It was well said by an Italian scholar: "The soul does not wax old" — *Anima non senescit.* You are not all the while praising former times and finding fault with the present. You are hopeful about the rising generation, and they are glad that you tarry among them. They love to behold one who is tolerant; who is serene and cheerful; who grows every year calmer and riper. If there is a little loss to the outer man, there is much gain to the spiritual man. Though one is growing less agile he may be growing more wise. We, younger folks, look upon such as invaluable depositaries of knowledge and experience; and we like to present drafts where they are always honored. Something besides years must be brought forward in proof that one has lived long; otherwise it is merely staying awhile. We are only receiving, not giving gifts; we have nothing but gratitude and love to offer. There are some plants that open only toward evening; and there are some trees from which we do not get the full benefit till frost begins to act upon their products. With you this is the mild Indian Summer of life.

You have not made living the great object of life, as Cornaro did; and so he continued over a hundred years; but what else did he do? Little besides teaching one good lesson, the value of temperance and geniality. When he set about regaining health which had been lost in middle life, his first object, he tells us, was the regulation of his temper, and the cultivation of cheerful habits. The Rev. Daniel Waldo, who lived to the age of one hundred and two, in giving advice to young men, said, among other things: "Go to your food, to your rest, to your occupations smiling. Keep a good nature and a soft temper everywhere." Cheerfulness and good health usually go hand in hand; so do cheerfulness and longevity, as in your own case; for the same spiritual regimen that favors the one, favors the other. Your movement, my friend, is not down hill, but upward. No one is superannuated till experience ceases to be of value. We are tempted to wish you might live as long as the phœnix; but that is not your wish; you have a very large interest in the next world, and where the treasure is there will the heart be also. You have reminded me of what the mother of Philip Henry, when quite advanced, remarked: "My head is in heaven, and my heart is in heaven; it is but one step more and I shall be there too."

> "Hope is singing, singing sweetly,
>   Softly in an undertone,
> Singing e'en as God has taught it—
>   'It is better further on!'

> "Further on; but how much further?
>   Count the mile stones one by one?
> No, no counting, only trusting—
>   'It is better further on!'"

XVIII.

To My Beloved Pupil,

A Happy New Year!

Happiest of the happy! such may you be. Does it seem to you that your teacher is sometimes exacting? You may be sure that any apparent severity has been consistent with the wish now uttered, and has sprung from an honest desire for your welfare.

Good manners have received attention, and I need not say, are of high importance to one's own comfort, and as a means of comfort and usefulness to others. To be rough and careless — neither of which is chargeable upon you — is the occasion of much needless pain. Genuine politeness is benevolence in little things; and the person who despises or disregards small courtesies, is ill-bred, if not ill-natured. A Chinese proverb says that " Ceremony is the smoke of friendship," but ceremonious manners at school or at home, are not the best manners. The golden rule lies at the base of good breeding. The way a thing is done, may sometimes be quite as important as what is done. It has been said that the Duke of

Marlborough gained more by the grace of his refusals, than most men do by granting favors. To be unmannered is unfortunate, to be ill-mannered is blameworthy.

An eye has been kept upon the formation of good mental habits, as one chief aim in education. Laziness, for instance, and happiness do not chum together. To have all the faculties in hand, and to use them with a will, at proper hours, is like the joyous exhilaration of robust play. Dawdling is twin sister to ennui, and is the mother of misery.

Shirking, whatever the method, is for the school, what counterfeiting or embezzlement is in the business world. To the dungeon with both of them! An honest, noble-minded youth despises every artifice for appearing to be a better scholar than he is. To quicken and concentrate the faculties for energetic harmonious exercise, has been a constant purpose. Looking upon the mind, not as a cask to be filled, but as an engine to be put in motion, I have always held cramming in detestation; and I have a deep sympathy with the little girl, of whom her schoolmistress inquired: "How is it, my dear, that you do not understand this simple thing?" "I have so many things to learn," she answered, "that I have no time to understand." To get together a mere heap of facts, or a mass of other men's ideas, falls short of the highest end, as truly as a pile of bricks comes short of being a beautiful edifice. It is sad to find so little difference, as we sometimes do, between a student and a book. The whole inner man, and the whole outer man — heart, head, and hand, trained to prompt, easy, well-balanced, well-directed work,— is the ideal; but it is not usual. If it were possible to have the higher mathematics or the learning of Greek made easy, high mental discipline cannot be made easy; and inertia is very apt to carry the day, for

> " To follow foolish precedents, and wink
> With both our eyes, is easier than to think."

You are one of the pupils whom I have never seen relapsing into listlessness, nor into carelessness, and I give you joy at the fact. You did once protest that you were extremely dull; but a real dunce never makes that discovery. Some of the most distinguished men and women seemed rather stupid, at least not particularly bright, in their school days. That was true of Sir Isaac Newton. The father of Dr. Isaac Barrow, in the bitterness of his heart, expressed the wish, that if it should please God to take away either of his children, it might be this unhopeful son. After receiving the rudiments of education, Sir Humphrey Davy was placed with a surgeon and apothecary, who pronounced him an idle and incorrigible boy. The Duke of Wellington's mother regarded him early as the dunce of the family, and was rather indifferent to his education; and Sheridan's mother, too, deemed him the most hopeless of her children on the score of intellect. Mistress Elizabeth Delap, who taught for more than half a century, had the honor of first putting a book into the hands of Oliver Goldsmith; but she had to confess that he was the dullest boy she ever dealt with, and that she sometimes doubted whether it would be possible to make anything of him. Douglas Jerrold was at first thought to be a heavy boy; so was Erasmus; and he certainly discovered no taste for literature, nor aptitude for its acquisition. Herder's teacher advised his father to bind him out to some mechanical employment.

However intense Scottish genius may be, *perfervidum ingenium Scotorum*, it is sometimes late in kindling. Thomson, author of the *Seasons*, was regarded as an inferior boy at school, and Thomas Chalmers was at the foot of his class. Barthold Niebuhr in his youth visited Edinburgh, and in one of his letters mentioned commiseratingly, that the eldest son in the Scott family was "dull in appearance and intellect;" but he became Sir Walter.

Many a diamond has a rough coating. A Rabbi once said: "I have learned much from my masters, more from companions, most of all from my scholars." It is from pupils that I have learned the most precious lessons of

the value of patient labor, and of hopefulness in spite of
unpromising early tokens.

" I remember the gleams and the glooms that dart
    Across the schoolboy's brain ;
The song and the silence in the heart,
That in part are prophecies, and in part
    Are longings wild and vain.
        And the voice of that fitful song
        Sings on and is never still :
        ' A boy's will is the wind's will,
And the thoughts of youth are long, long thoughts.' "

—81—

XIX.

To My Faithful Teacher,

A HAPPY NEW YEAR!

MOST cordial is the wish. I am greatly your debtor. A sincere salutation today will not indeed do anything toward payment; but the least I can do is to make acknowledgment, and to cherish the hope that a rich harvest of satisfaction may be enjoyed as you recall the patience, fidelity, and tact shown in your treatment of pupils. Alexander the Great used to say that he owed less to Philip, his father, for birth, than to Aristotle, his master, for a good education, inasmuch as it is less to live than to live well. But was he not a better pupil than son; and was it not due to the father that he had so excellent a teacher? I have no occasion to make comparisons of that kind, but I have occasion to cherish gratitude and affection for one, with whom stands associated so much that is pleasing and valuable in the period and place of study.

I desire to thank you most earnestly for those wise maxims which you often repeated, and on which you acted, so far as the dullness and perversity of pupils did not prevent, especially these : The method of study is no less important than what is studied ; To find out is solid cash, to be told is only a promise to pay; To be told will keep you a boy, to be trained will make you a man ; Don't study for the recitation, but for the life-time; This is not a Chinese school for training memory alone ; A well-stored mind may be an ill-balanced mind ; The mind must be a fountain, not a mere reservoir ; Persons may be thoroughly instructed and yet not educated ; The most agreeable thing is to master the disagreeable.

You once pointed out the passage in which Plato says that what he meant by education was condensed into one word, *Discipline ;* and another dictum of his : "The wise man requires seven years to seize the ideas, and fourteen to learn how to adapt them to reality." Well do I remember your citing the incident of an Irish pupil. "The first half dozen lessons are tedious and disagreeable," said his German teacher, "after that you will begin to appreciate the beauties of the language." "Then," said the young son of Erin, "suppose we begin at the seventh at once." You used to say : Thorough discipline makes heroes ; and now and then would repeat what Lord Wellington said in his old age, when on a visit to the place of his training : "Yes, yes, it was at Eton that Waterloo was won."

Not unfrequently there were grave moral sayings. I often think of this: "Poor student! who knows everything, and does nothing — nothing for his kindred, nothing for his neighborhood." One day you brought in the *Life of Southey*, and read this: "After all, knowledge is not the first thing needful. Provided we can get contentedly through the world and to heaven at last, the sum of knowledge we may collect on the way is more infinitely insignificant than I like to acknowledge in my own heart." This, too, was dropped occasionally: "Alas for the education in which nothing is neglected but religion!" You convinced us that no amount of genius or acquisitions would make any one happy. We were reminded that Dean Swift, one of the most talented and one of the most selfish of men, was pronounced by Archbishop King, "The most unhappy man on earth."

At the close of each term we were reminded that there is a great examination day at hand, when the chief question will be, not how much we know of history, of language, of natural science, but whether we have loved God with all the heart, and have believed in Jesus Christ, and have been his disciples. A thousand thanks that in all your talks about favorite authors, you still left the impression upon pupils that the Bible is the one book from heaven, and the one guide-book to heaven.

They all, I believe, at your suggestion learned these
lines of Sir Walter Scott:

> " Within that awful volume lies
> The mystery of mysteries.
> Happiest they, of human race,
> To whom our God has given grace
> To read, to fear, to hope, to pray,
> To lift the latch, and force the way ;
> And better had they ne'er been born
> Who read to doubt, or read to scorn."

XX.

To My Industrious Friend,

A HAPPY NEW YEAR!

YOU seem, my friend, to have no leisure for being unhappy. Ennui has no chance to get hold of you, for work is your choice and your pleasure. I have never heard you sigh over waste of time or the want of time, for you have all there is of it, and all that can be had. Persevering toil in some line of honest effort is indispensable to mental health and enjoyment. Solomon was right: "The sleep of the laboring man is sweet." No man, primitive or in our day, was ever put into Paradise, except on this, as one condition, "to dress it and to keep it." Divine authority enjoins rest on the seventh day no more than labor on the other six days.

You will agree with me that the great men of the world have been great workers; and when they have kept from overdoing, have, other things equal, experienced delight in occupation as such. "It is a most royal thing to labor," said Alexander the Great. The shrewd and indefatigable Ferdinand of Castile and Arragon, like thousands of others, found repose in change of work, but it was work still. "Let others take the riches," said Melancthon; "give me the work." What a robust toiler, and what a cheery man was Martin Luther, carrying out the old artist's maxim: "No day without a line"— *Nulla dies sine linea*. Life is often a running commentary on a man's maxim or motto, as was Sir Walter Scott's "Never to be doing nothing," and Voltaire's *Toujours au travail*, "Always at work." Seldom has there been a more industrious or happier man than John Wesley, who declared, "Leisure and I have taken leave of one another." "I have lived," said Dr. Adam Clarke, "to know that the great secret of human happiness is this — never suffer your energies to stagnate. The old adage of 'too many irons in the fire,' conveys an untruth. You cannot have too many; poker, tongs, and all — keep them all going." "We are all bees here — busy and happy," said Mary Lyon at Mt. Holyoke Seminary. Woe to the community when idleness supplants industry! You recollect how bees that were taken to the Barbadoes, finding the materials for honey so plentiful and the climate so fine at all seasons, ceased to lay up stores after the first year, became demoralized, and took to flying about the sugar-houses and stinging the negroes. They had turned aristocrats, acting on the idea that labor is degrading, and that the world owed them a living. They illustrated the fact that one may be busy without being industrous; that a busy man is not necessarily a man of business.

Of all miserable creatures, who is more so than the one who "eats the bread of idleness," whose unpaid poll-tax is due in Apragapolis, a city void of business? Idlers are "fools at large," lounging at street corners, in the shop, in the bar-room, aimless good-for-nothings. As they have nothing of any importance to do, they succeed in that and in nothing else. The chief specimen of activity which they furnish, is with the lower section of the head, the masticating machine.

The Arabs have a proverb: "The idle are a peculiar kind of dead, who cannot be buried." Without honorable employment no one can be sure of not sinking into hypochondria. What excellent advice it was that Dr. Abernethy gave to a rich valetudinarian in London: "Live on a shilling a day, and earn it." When the friends of Count Caylies asked him why he spent so much time in engraving the plates for his valuable antiquarian works, he replied: "I engrave lest I should hang myself"—*Je grave pour ne pas me pendre;* and Napoleon, hearing at St. Helena of the death of an old friend, a Colonel, asked: "Of what disease?" "That of having nothing to do," was the reply. "Enough," said he, "even if he had been an emperor."

Happy New Year!

You, my friend, agree with me that this world is not a great play-ground ; but a place for earnestness and industry ; and that the doom, "In the sweat of thy face shalt thou eat bread," carries in it a large element of loving-kindness. Holy angels are never idle. Those whom Jacob saw on the ladder were not standing still. "Are they not all ministering spirits?" You have noticed that God's special visits and special favors are in no instance to idlers. His memorable manifestation to Gideon was at the threshing floor, and to Moses, David, and the shepherds at Bethlehem, when they were tending their flocks. "Seest thou a man diligent in his business; he shall stand before kings." "I can attest the truth of that," said Benjamin Franklin, "for I have transacted business with five monarchs in my time."

" Bring your axes, woodmen true;
Smite the forest till the blue
Of Heaven's sunny eye looks through
Every wild and tangled glade ;
Jungled swamp and thicket shade
    Give to day !
O'er the torrents fling your bridges,
Pioneers ! Upon the ridges,
Widen, smooth the rocky stair—

My Industrious Friend.

They that follow, far behind
Coming after us, will find
Surer, easier footing there;
Heart to heart, and hand with hand,
From the dawn till dusk of day,
    Work away!
Scouts upon the mountain's peak —
Ye that see the Promised Land,
Hearten us! for ye can speak
Of the country ye have scanned
    Far away!"

XXI.

To My Punctual Friend.

A HAPPY NEW YEAR!

IF you were not habitually punctual, I could hardly give you this greeting, for it would be an idle wish. How can any one who is uniformly tardy be happy? Such must have an ill-regulated mind, or a dormant conscience, or both, and in any case must move on a low plane of enjoyment. What a miserable creature is the man or woman who was chasing lost half hours all through the last twelvemonth; and now, without overtaking a single one, chases them into this New Year's Day! And worse yet for one who is too indifferent to make the attempt; who is quietly careless about appointments with himself and with others. He is morally weak; he is dishonest, and deserves never to hear the congratulation, Happy New Year!

Would that an adequate penalty for tardiness were always administered! You remember Wellington was noted for his exactness in meeting engagements — who ever heard of a great general, or other really great man, that was not? — but the Iron Duke, once in his life, found himself behind time. It was at Lady Jersey's party. The announcement being made: "Lady Jersey, the Duke of Wellington is at the door, and desires to be admitted." "What o'clock is it?" she asked. "Seven minutes after eleven, your ladyship." She paused a moment, and then said: "Give Lady Jersey's compliments to the Duke of Wellington, and say that she is very glad that the first enforcement of the rule of exclusion is such, that hereafter no one can complain of its application. He cannot be admitted." In the battle of Waterloo, Blücher was punctual at Mont St. Jean; Grouchy was not, and so the allies won the day.

"Punctuality, *exactitude*, is the politeness of kings," said Louis XVIII of France. Queen Victoria, as you are aware, is noted for that habit, though it may now and then show itself in a somewhat imperial way. On one state occasion the Duchess of Sutherland, whose place was near her majesty, kept the royal party waiting for a quarter of an hour. The Queen was just about to enter her carriage without the first lady of honor, when the latter made her appearance out of breath. "My dear Duchess," said the Queen, "I think you must have a bad watch," at the same time passing her own chain, with a costly time-keeper, around the neck of Lady Sutherland. This will remind you of Washington's habit, and particularly of what he said to Hamilton, when, in a second instance of failing to meet the General punctually, he laid the blame on his watch. "Then," said Washington, "you must either get a new watch, or I must get a new secretary." George III, too, was extremely punctual. Did you ever meet with the incident of a certain Lord and the hall clock? His Lordship, who prided himself on exactness, had an appointment with the king one day at Windsor Castle. While passing through the hall he heard the clock strike twelve, whereupon with his cane he broke the face of the faithful monitor. At the next audience the king exclaimed: "Why, how came you to strike the clock?" "The clock struck first, your majesty," was the ready answer.

One great secret of success, on the part of many eminent men, is their exact observance of appointments. Melancthon would have not only the hour but the minute fixed, that neither he nor others might suffer loss or suspense. For more than thirty years the philosopher Kant rose precisely at the same minute. "I never saw," says Dr. J. W. Alexander, "a perfectly punctual scholar go astray."

Studious and literary men, you must have noticed, often have such a habit of being absorbed as to be insensible to the lapse of time. Cowper confesses that he "never knew a poet except himself, who was punc-

tual in anything." Yet Wordsworth, as a distributer of
stamps, and Scott, as Clerk to the Court of Session,
showed themselves prompt business men. So did Chau-
cer, Spenser and Milton. Sir Isaac Newton, in the office
of Master of the Mint, distinguished himself for exactness as to hours, no less than any other man in govern-
ment service. Blackstone, when delivering his law lect-
ures, was never known to keep his audience waiting
for an instant; and Lord Brougham, with all his multifarious public engagements, was uniformly punctual
in meeting them.

"Never" — so wrote William Cobbett — "never did
any man or anything wait one moment for me." A vast
amount of reasonable enjoyment falls to the person who
can say that. He has a quiet conscience, at least on one
point. And you, my friend, I am glad to congratulate
as one happy in this gratifying habit. None can charge
you with robbing them of time — a robbery which neither
thief nor loser can restore. It has been no small satisfaction to me to hear you say, more than once : If a man
has a right to waste his own time, he has no right to
waste mine; and also : As one cannot overtake a lost
quarter of an hour, he should manage to keep a little
before it.

A coachman said to Nelson, when on the eve of
departure for one of his great expeditions: "The car-

riage shall be at your door at six o'clock." "A quarter before," said Nelson; "I have always been a quarter of an hour before my time, and it has made a man of me." The tardy man, whether in business, politics, or war, is foredoomed to defeat and to misery. Let an hour-glass be put into his coffin, and be buried with him.

Some men's movements can be depended on not less than the movements of the clock. John Quincy Adams was such a one. Even in advanced age he was usually among the first members of Congress to take his seat at the Capitol, in the morning, and was the last to leave it. On one occasion a member said to the Speaker: "It is time to call this house to order." "No," said the Speaker, "Mr. Adams is not yet in his place." The next moment the old man eloquent entered, and the House was at once called to order. Other men can be depended on also for one thing, and that is that they will not be punctual. You can be perfectly sure they will not be on time. There are certain mechanics on whom you can rely for not having their work ready when it is promised; and certain attendants upon public worship who are equally reliable. They seem to have no conscience about robbing God or man. "Bringeth forth his fruit in his season," is the Scripture authority which Miss Mary Lyon used to adduce for punctuality. Oh! for more good women like the one who said, when asked why she was always at church before the hour: "It is no part of my religion to disturb the religion of others." Have you ever known a man habitually unpunctual, whose integrity in other respects could be relied upon? In China all debts must be paid on their New Year's Day; in default of which business must close. Is the promise to do a certain thing at a given time, any less a contract than is a promise to pay? If careless about the one, is it presumable a man will not be careless about the other? Is not time money, and more than money?

Joy to you, once more, my friend, that you are not a loiterer; that you never by tardiness give opportunity for misfortune; that you never needlessly fail to meet engagements, any more than the earth we inhabit fails to get around in her orbit at the right time and place, every New Year's morning! Here are lines that you know by heart:

> " Hoist up sail while gale doth last,
>   Tide and wind wait no man's pleasure;
> Seek not time when time is past;
>   Sober speed is wisdom's leisure:
> After-wits are dearly bought,
> Let thy fore-wit guide thy thought."

XXII.

To My Young Student Friend,

A HAPPY NEW YEAR!

A DOUBLY happy New Year may it be. You are a favored one. You have, in some good measure, opportunity for gratifying a strong and praiseworthy desire. It gives me great satisfaction to see you so earnestly bent on mental improvement, and enjoying so much in your pursuits. You remind me of what the studious Lady Jane Grey said, as she looked out upon those devoted to the chase: "I wist that all their sport in the park is but a shadow to that pleasure that I find in Plato. Alas! good folk, they never felt what true pleasure meant." Young as she was, she had acquired, as do all who have well-regulated minds, the habit of thorough study. Constant, rapid, and miscellaneous reading, especially in early life, is destructive to vigorous and symmetrical culture. Getting information is the less important part of education; wise discipline of the faculties is the chief thing. Digestion takes time; overtasking the organs brings on dyspepsia. One may become very fat without being strong at all. So then, let your older friend make a suggestion or two.

For one thing, avoid a languid use of books. Listlessness in reading or study, dozing over a lesson, or merely going over so much ground as a stint, is, like all other shams, a miserable method. It will lead to utter mental shiftlessness and torpor. Sir Thomas Fowell Buxton carried out three maxims: "Never to begin a book without finishing it;" "never to consider a book finished until it was mastered;" and "to study everything with the whole mind." Jeremiah Evarts, in his fifth year, came to his father for a new book, who asked if the last one he had given him was worn out. "Oh, no, sir," said the boy, "but I have read all the sense out of it." By such a habit one has his knowledge about him, instead of only knowing that certain books contain it for him; and he might say, as Valcourt did when his library was burned up: "A man must have profited very little by his books, who has not learned how to part with them." You have met with the old Latin proverb, *Cave ab homine unius libri* — "Beware of the man of one book." Ponder this too, *Multum non multa* — "Much, not many."

You will find it a helpful practice to have some favorite author, or at most a few such, and read and re-read them as long as you live. Sir William Jones invariably read through the works of Cicero every year, and the celebrated Bourdaloue did the same, but he also went through Chrysostom, St. Paul and St. John.

With all your ardor, which is so promising, do not be sanguine about mastering the whole circuit of human knowledge. Think of the literature in many foreign languages. Think of the treasures in our own language. Out of half a million, or possibly a million volumes, probably not over fifty thousand are worth perusal. If you were able to go through that mass of reading at the rate of one book a day, you would need to live over a hundred and thirty years from this time onward. Take the library of the British Museum alone, which occupies ten miles of shelf. Supposing it to be arranged according to a wise method of examination, and you should require only one day for each book, large or small, you would need to live longer than Methuselah to reach the farther end. You are taken aback, and it is indeed rather humiliating. I by no means wish to check your eagerness in the pursuit of knowledge, but I do desire to have you saved from exaggerated expectations.

And then let me remind you of what Milton says:

" Deep versed in books, but shallow in himself."

Acquaintance with yourself, that indispensable department of knowledge, is not to be had by multifarious reading. What am I? Why am I here? Whither am

I going? are good questions for New Year's Day. It occurs to me that as some friends of Barnes, a seventeenth century divine, were praising his library, he said: "Ay, there stand my books, but the Lord knows that for many years last past, I have studied my heart more than my books."

I am rejoiced to know that you shun immoral works, and that you have but a slight taste for works of fiction. I trust that you will keep it in mind that the great aim should be, not so much to become learned as wise; and that devotion to reading and study, while far above all grovelling pleasures, may yet be only a form of refined selfishness. "I carried along with me," said Sir Matthew Hale, "in all my studies this great design, namely, of improving them, and the knowledge acquired by them for the honor of God's name, and the greater discovery of his wisdom, power and truth; and so translated my secular learning into an improvement of divine knowledge." "One devout thought," said Archbishop Leighton, pointing to his books, "is worth them all."

> " Knowledge is proud that he has learned so much;
> Wisdom is humble that he knows no more.
> Books are not seldom talismans and spells,
> By which the magic arts of shrewder wits
> Hold an unthinking multitude enthralled.
> Some to the fascination of a name

My Young Student Friend.

Surrender judgment hoodwinked. Some the style
Infatuates, and through labyrinth and wilds
Of error leads them, by a tune entranced.
While sloth seduces more, too weak to bear
The insupportable fatigue of thought,
And swallowing therefore without pause or choice
The total grist unsifted, husks and all."

XXIII.

To My Aspiring Friend,

A HAPPY NEW YEAR!

I DO not wish to flatter you, but I do wish, with the usual congratulations of the season, to congratulate you on the high aims which you have formed. You propose not to be content with ordinary attainments in self-culture, in the skill and the results appropriate to that line of things which you have chosen. Sir James Stephen, Professor of Modern History in the University of Cambridge, and whose name ranks high in the English literature of our century, said in a lecture before the Young Men's Christian Association of London: "If, in virtue of having numbered more years than most of my audience, I might presume to speak as the monitor of those whom I address, my whole exhortation to them might be comprised in a single word; and that one word would be — A S P I R E !" He adds a quotation from George Herbert:

> "Pitch thy behavior low, thy projects high;
> So shalt thou humble and magnanimous be.

Happy New Year!

> Sink not in spirit; who aimeth at the sky,
> Shoots higher much, than he that means a tree."

You have read and observed enough to know that the men who accomplish much for society, do not stumble into excellence, but work hard. They are not addicted to castle-building; they form definite purposes, not mere general purposes, and they keep steadfast to their aim. Think of Wedgwood, who would not tolerate inferior work, and was never satisfied till he had done his best. If a manufactured article did not come up to his idea of what it should be, he would dash it in pieces, saying: "This won't do for Josiah Wedgwood." What an enviable reputation was that of Ulfilas, Bishop of the Goths, away back in the fourth century! It became a proverb among his rude people, "Whatever Ulfilas does is well done."

> " Longings sublime and aspirations high."

These might take the form of idle, selfish ambition; but I trust that with you it is something better; that there is a strong desire to do as well as possible, because it is wrong to do otherwise; because it is unworthy of a rational being to be content with a low standard. If you look into the *Memoir of Baron Bunsen* you will find this record relating to a noble group of students at Göttingen in 1813: "A spirit of zealous but friendly emulation

arose amongst us ; and on a certain cheerful evening, at
my suggestion, we made a vow, each to each other and
to all, that we would effect something great in our lives."
There were five of them originally, to whom three others
were added, and the pledge was not a vain one. This
may remind you of five English young men, who, on one
occasion, jointly and solemnly resolved "to make the
most of life." They too kept their vow — Ryland distinguished himself as teacher of theological students, Fuller
as a theological writer, Carey as a Bible translator, while
Sutcliffe and Pearce became pastors of no ordinary excellence.

What need is there that anybody should be a nobody,
simply getting through life after a fashion, contentedly
lethargic, lazily indifferent to what he was made for, and
what he has to account for? The grass might just as well
be already growing over such. Scarcely less pitiable are
those who bustle about, with no well defined object, in a
vain and vague activity, like Lord Viscount Barrington,
who was described as a little squirrel of state, busy all
his life in the cage, without turning it round to any human purpose. It is not indeed for all to become great ;
and mere greatness is a small matter. Your object, your
motive is the main thing. "Power to do good," says
Lord Bacon, "is the only true and lawful end of aspir-
ing ;" and who cannot compass that? Success therein

puts one into the aristocracy — the élite of a kingdom on which the sun will never set, even when this earth and all the works therein shall be burned up. Feeble powers, scant culture, humble position, want of money cannot keep one from standing high in the divine esteem; "Whosoever of you will be the chiefest, shall be servant of all."

To live for Christ, and to live like Christ is the highest aim and the purest joy possible. Anything less for one's supreme purpose is too low. "What will you now do with your astronomy?" said an intimate friend, to a man devoted to that science, but who had become a servant of the Lord Jesus. "I am now bound for heaven," said he, "and I take the stars in my way."

> " Higher and yet more high !
> Shake off the cumbering chain which earth would lay
> On your victorious wings ; mount, mount ! Your way
> Is through eternity ! "

XXIV.

To My Friend in Public Life,

A HAPPY NEW YEAR!

You will have many congratulations today, and you are entitled to them. The community joins in good wishes, and not a few will be most sincere and appreciative. But your position will also suggest —

> " That flattering crowds officiously appear,
>   To give themselves, not you, a happy year ;
>   And by the greatness of their presents prove
>   How much they hope, but not how well they love."

You have not read history in vain. It is a good while since you became convinced that mere place can make no one happy, and I do not need to refresh your recollection with illustrative instances. Your memory will at once range up and down among the crowned heads and statesmen of different lands. Gibbon's record of what the Caliph Abdalrahman said will come to mind : " I have now reigned above fifty years, in victory or peace, beloved by my subjects, dreaded by my enemies,

and respected by my allies. Riches and honors, power and
pleasure, have waited on my call, nor does any earthly
blessing appear to have been wanting to my felicity. In
this situation I have diligently numbered the days of
pure and genuine happiness which have fallen to my lot;
they amount to fourteen. O man! place not thy confidence in the present world!" It would be interesting —
would it not? — to know just which those fourteen days
were, an average of less than one in a thousand, and
what it was that made them exceptional. How well did
Henry IV of France reply to a courtier who was descant-
ing on the happiness of kings: " They are not so happy
as you imagine them to be. Kings are either bad or
good men. If they are bad men, they bear within themselves their own plague and torment. If they are good
men, they find from other people a thousand causes of
uneasiness and affliction. A good king feels the misfor-
tunes of all his subjects, and in a great kingdom, what
innumerable sources are there of affliction." What an
unhappy man was Frederick the Great! Even Bonaparte confessed that the most enjoyable part of his life
was when he was a poor lieutenant. Wilberforce, who
knew William Pitt intimately, says that he died of a
broken heart. A man must be very miserable to be so
gruff as Lord Melville was one morning, though high in
office, and the idol of his Scottish countrymen. Sir John

Sinclair, his guest at the time, repaired early to the room of the statesman, to wish him a Happy New Year. "It had need to be happier than the last," said his lordship, "for I cannot recollect a single happy day in it."

Public men are seldom willing to have it known how many annoyances they meet with — the petty carping of petty men, the ill-natured criticisms of the disappointed and the envious, as well as the calumnies of unprincipled opponents. One can hardly help thinking of the adage, more expressive than elegant: "He gets honey too dear who licks it from thorns." I have often heard you speak of the uncertainties of popular favor and of place. That indeed is a running title on the annals of every nation. The acclamations and splendor of any great occasion, remind us of the answer given by a monarch to a courtier who accompanied him amidst the pomp of a triumphal procession, and who asked: "What is wanting here?" "Continuance is wanting."

But the man who, like yourself, is governed by principle, who has fixedness of purpose in doing what is right, who serves the community with a genuine public spirit, whose patriotism is pure enough not to require protestation from himself, or indorsement from others, is a great benediction and a power. All hearts worth having, and all good wishes gravitate toward him. No executive energy, nor sharpness of intellect, nor splendor of eloquence, will avail, if unswerving integrity do not preside over the whole, and no uprightness can be depended upon for every emergency if it have not a religious basis. "He that walketh righteously, and speaketh uprightly; he that despiseth the gains of oppression, that shaketh his hands from holding of bribes, he shall dwell on high; his place of defence shall be the munitions of rocks." Such a man is always in office, always on the throne of public confidence, and no party changes can cast him down.

> "Statesman, yet friend to truth; of soul sincere;
> In action faithful, and in honor clear;
> Who broke no promise, served no private end;
> Who gained no title, and who lost no friend."

XXV.

To My Faithful Pastor,

A HAPPY NEW YEAR!

IF you are as happy as some of your flock today, you begin the year with no small amount of joy. "Blessed are they who do hunger and thirst after righteousness," and blessed are they who help to supply the food required. Your hearers get something besides husks from the pulpit, something besides soft and sentimental utterances, something besides aimless and characterless sermons; they have what they need, not only "the sincere milk of the Word," but "strong meat" also. Our pastorate is filled by one who evidently seeks our edification rather than our admiration, who thinks more of usefulness than greatness. "Woe and anathema," says Luther, "to all those preachers who love to handle lofty, difficult and subtle questions in the pulpit, and bring such before the common people, and enlarge upon them, seeking their own honor and glory." I think you would much rather preach the everlasting gospel than be the angel who is to sound the last trump.

Thanks that false tenderness does not take all point out of your preaching; that your pulpit is not a "Coward's Castle;" that boldness in sin meets with boldness of reproof; that sin is treated not so much as a misfortune as a crime; that you teach what the Bible teaches — that something more than help is needed; that the great sacrificial work of Jesus Christ is indispensable, and the renewing energy of the ever blessed Spirit of God. Your discourses come manifestly from some other source than the sermon-mill; no one suspects that the sacred office has been assumed "by constraint;" and it must be evident to all that you preach Christ for Christ's own sake.

Dr. John Brown of Edinburgh relates that, after hearing his great grandfather preach, David Hume said: "That's the man for me; he means what he says; he speaks as if Jesus Christ was at his elbow." You are familiar with what John Brown of Haddington, who belonged to the same family, said — and no doubt your heart responds Amen to it — "After all I dare not but confess Christ to be the best Master I ever served. Often in preaching and otherwise, I have found his words 'the joy and rejoicing of my heart.' . . . And now after near forty years' preaching of Christ and his great and sweet salvation, I think that if God were to renew my youth, and put it entirely in my choice, whether I would be

king of Great Britain, or a preacher of the Gospel with
'the Holy Ghost sent down from Heaven,' who had to
beg his bread all the laboring days of the week, in order
to have an opportunity of preaching on the Sabbath to
an assembly of sinful men, I would, by his grace, never
hesitate a moment to make my choice." Such ministers
— and not those who administer an opiate divinity, nor
the aspirants for pulpit favor, nor the race of clerical
cossets — are the happy ministers. It is men like Ober-
lin of Steinthal, who could speak so freely yet unosten-
tatiously, of his filial fear and love toward God, and
in reply to a direct question, could say: "Yes, I *am*
happy!"

Nor are your good sermons on the Sabbath spoiled by
a poor life between Sabbaths. Your prompt, kind and
faithful ministrations to the sick, the bereaved, and the
heavy-laden, bring untold comfort and relief. Paul was
not the only one who could appeal to his flock: "Ye
are my witnesses, and God also, how holily, and justly,
and unblamably we behaved ourselves among you that
believe; as ye know how we exhorted and comforted,
and charged every one of you, as a father doth his
children." When Venn preached his farewell sermon,
weeping mothers held up their children, saying: "There
is the man who has been our most faithful minister and
our best friend." May I never hear a farewell sermon

from my beloved pastor! I hope that your study door
may have such a paper on the inside as the Rev. Thomas
Adam of Wintringham left on his: " To my successor:
Whoever thou art, who enterest here, if thou hast
found the life of thy own soul, faith and conversion,
and comest here to attend thy charge, and with an
earnest will to serve the Lord Jesus Christ in the min-
istry, this place will be a Paradise to thee."

> " Unpracticed he to fawn or seek for power,
> By doctrines fashioned to the varying hour ;
> Far other aims his heart had learned to prize,
> More skilled to raise the wretched than to rise."

XXVI.

To My Beloved People,

A HAPPY NEW YEAR!

THIS salutation is a supplication, that the first day
of the year, and all following days, may find you happy —
happy in person and estate, in relations and occupations !
Our planet has been once more on her long annual pil-
grimage, traversing broad fields of space, but has reached
the goal again; and fain would I present you at this dawn
of a new year with a greeting, that shall make winter smile
like a summer morning.

Grace be to you, and peace ! — grace from Him who
is the same yesterday, and today, and forever, the Great
Shepherd and Bishop of souls; the grace that shall
bring spiritual health and growth ; the grace that shall
cause abundant joy in the Holy Ghost, and that shall
give well grounded assurance of vital union to Him who
is the resurrection and the life. May ample peace be
yours — a quiet conscience, a calm Christian trust; the
absence of imagined evils and whatever tends to corrode
the heart, and the presence of that which can make

men sing even in prison, and at midnight. May all the elements essential to true happiness be in your possession — all those pure motives and high aims that sink self out of sight, and lead to a vigorous practice of Christian activities; that beget a generous and abiding impulse to make the most of life for the benefit of others, both near at hand and far away. As pastor and personal friend of all, those older and those younger, my prayer is that, in spite of apprehensions, temptations and assaults, you may come off more than conquerors, and maintain blameless living; that if any should be called to an experience in the burning fiery furnace, they may there find One like unto the Son of God, standing by them more evidently than at any other time; that the year now opening with many good wishes, may close with more giving of thanks for unprecedented benefits from on high.

The Romans deemed New Year's Day to be a sign-day, a leading or governing day, that any affair which proved successful then, was to be taken as a good omen for the whole twelvemonth. The late Dr. James W. Alexander mentioned to a friend: "For the coming year I have fixed on the year-word, 'God with us.' This method of year motto I have pursued now for about fifteen years, with much comfort to my own heart, and I believe to others; especially as I have preached on the text whenever I had a congregation." I commend to each of you a similar adoption of some pertinent passage of Holy Writ — a pocket-piece, that shall be constantly at hand as a monitor and sacred talisman.

There is one transaction which never fails to be propitious on the Kalends of January — the renewed presentation of one's self heartily, wholly and forever, a living sacrifice unto Him whose we are, and whom it is our high privilege to serve. A passage not inappropriate for myself, is the apostolic paradox: "As poor, yet making many rich." Gladly would I, an almoner on earth for our Lord on high, come to you with hands loaded from the great storehouse of blessings — with manna and the cup of cold water, with the pearl of great price — and so aid all in laying up treasures in heaven.

It is not yours but you, not the fleece but the flock that I covet. To win souls to Christ is to enrich them, and to enrich his kingdom, beyond the wealth of Crœsus. "I would think," said Matthew Henry — and for what true minister does he not speak? — "I would think it a greater happiness to gain one soul to Christ, than mountains of gold and silver to myself." "I pronounce it with the greatest sincerity," said the sweet singer whose sacred songs we employ in larger number than any other man's, "that there is no place, or company, or employment this side heaven, which can give me such a relish of delight as when I stand ministering in holy things in the midst of you."

Not without some measure of sympathy do I quote what Dr. Chalmers penned one first day of January: "Let me lay myself out for the happiness of those around me, and make every sacrifice, whether of vanity or indolence, to the perfect fulfillment of Christian love." With a New Year's prayer of Thomas Becon in the sixteenth century, I close: "God, the Author of every year, vouchsafe to grant that this New Year, with many others, may ever begin unto you prosperously, proceed better, end with that which is best, and always be prosperous unto you so long as they last, so that you may alway enjoy continual health and prosperous felicity, according to the will of God, to whom be all honor and glory. Amen."

XXVII.

To My Bereaved Friend,

V

A HAPPY NEW YEAR!

I AM mindful, my dear friend, of that on which your thoughts dwell so much. Do not think me wanting in sensibility or in sympathy. A tear comes to my eye while this wish is on my tongue.

I believe — and I know you believe — there is such a thing as "sorrowful, yet alway rejoicing;" and that a happy New Year's Day is more than possible to one in deep affliction. God's Word and his gracious presence show that this is not an insoluble paradox. "Behold, happy is the man whom God correcteth" — happy in the thought that it is no less his right to take than to give; and that when he appoints a bereavement, it must be better than the presence of the loved one. We do not dare to sit in judgment on his fatherly chastisements. What he gives in love to us, we would in love to him give back whenever he recalls; and that too, not in sheer submission to the inevitable, not in a hard, stoical or Mohammedan yielding to destiny, but in tender, filial acquiescence. One may feel deeply and yet be sweetly resigned. In the midst of tears comes the rainbow; and the darker the cloud the brighter the coloring. What reason is there to think that if I am not satisfied with God's will here, I shall be hereafter? And when there is good reason to believe that the object of affection is removed to a better world, is it not fitting that I should be more than resigned, that I should be positively joyful? John Newton says that he watched his dying wife some hours, with a candle in his hand, and when he was sure she had breathed her last — which could not at once be determined, she went away so easily — he knelt down and thanked the Lord for her dismission. "Hosanna! Hosanna in the highest!" wrote Lady Colquhoun; "I have just heard that my beloved Hannah is in glory! What cause for praise!"

God takes to give, to give himself in a fullness of joy. "God and enough," says a Welsh proverb. He lets his servants be put into a furnace, and then comes and stands very sensibly near them himself. You have seen and have read of persons who experience a profound and heavenly peace of soul in the midst of sore bereavements. The Rev. Andrew Fuller, when a child died — himself on a sick bed at the time — called his family around him, prayed and blessed "A taking as well as a giving God." Was it not wise in Mrs. Savage, sister of

Matthew Henry, to make this entry in her journal: "Resolved to call nothing mine but God?" At eighty-seven, and after forty years of widowhood, Lady Rachel Russell was able to say: "God hath not denied me the support of his Holy Spirit, in this my long day of calamity, but has enabled me in some measure to rejoice in him as my portion forever."

"And be it so, I know it well; myself and all that's mine,
Must roll on with the rolling year, and ripen to decline.
I do not shun the solemn truth, to him it is not drear,
        Whose hopes can rise
        Above the skies,
    And see a Saviour near.

"It only makes him feel with joy, this earth is not his home;
It sends him on from present ills to brighter hours to come;
It bids him take with thankful heart whate'er his God may send,
        Content to go
        Through weal and wo,
    To glory in the end."

XXVIII.

To My Widowed Friend,

A Happy New Year!

HAPPY it may be, though the cypress was planted
not long ago. Sure I am there is infinitely more left
than has been taken. You assent to this; and yet more,
it has your hearty endorsement. Your record is: " I
cried unto thee, O Lord! I said, Thou art my refuge
and my portion in the land of the living!"

Mourning there will be, but murmuring may have
no place in it. The morally enfeebling effects of exces-
sive grief you would earnestly shun. Was it not a
pitiable sight to see the Empress Maria Theresa go
down into the vault, every Friday for thirteen years
after her husband's death, to weep by the side of his
remains? "I am alone today, and in another world,"
wrote the widow of Herder, on the anniversary of his
decease. Heaven rather than the tomb, should attract
thoughts and steps. The winter and the weeds of
widowhood will then give place to the flowers of Paradise. Disproportionate meditation, however, even upon

blessedness above, and a prolonged seclusion are liable to prove unhealthful. The tonic of active beneficence is needed to preserve mental and spiritual balance and vigor. To think and talk largely about one's loneliness, without effective sympathy for others; to shed many tears over one's own trial, and do nothing to wipe away the tears of neighboring mourners, is, in your estimation, no part of genuine womanliness nor of Christian character. It is debilitating; it is itself a weakness. Aiming at eminence of grief is one of the least laudable and least remunerative forms of ambition.

"The pleasure of doing good," says a Chinese proverb, "is the only one that never wears out." The first time after the removal of her husband, that the neighbors saw Lady Colquhoun, except in church, was at the formation of a Bible Society, and that, too, only a few weeks subsequent to the trying event. Mary Bosanquet, for over thirty years the widow of that rare man, John William Fletcher, or Fléchère, found her delight in continued efforts to be useful to others. Lady Huntingdon had an experience of widowhood for forty-five years, but was uniformly cheerful and happy in the dedication of time, talents, and property to the support and diffusion of the gospel. "God brought me to himself by afflictions," said Lady Maxwell, whose husband, Walter Maxwell, Bart., died when she was but nineteen.

My Widowed Friend.

For more than half a century of widowhood — fifty-three
years — it was her unfailing joy to show sympathy for
the needy and distressed.   Although her resources,
especially in later life, were not large, yet she continued
constantly to aid numerous institutions of private and
public charity.   I know well, my dear friend, what your
purpose is.

> " Wouldst thou from sorrow find a sweet relief ?
> Or is thy heart oppressed with woes untold ?
> Balm wouldst thou gather for corroding grief ?
> Pour blessings round thee like a shower of gold ;
> 'Tis when the rose is wrapt in many a fold,
> Close to its heart, the worm is wasting there
> Its life and beauty ; not, when all unrolled,
> Leaf after leaf its bosom rich and fair
> Breathes freely its perfumes throughout the ambient air."

XXIX.

To My Suffering Friend,

A Happy New Year!

Yes, a Happy New Year's Day, in the midst of pain, and in spite of pain! There is no mockery in the wish. True happiness does not consist in agreeable sensations; it comes as a gracious gift from God, and it will spring out of sweet resignation to his trying appointments; out of filial delight in him as the All-wise Father. To do his will lies largely in bearing his will. These pains are severe teachers, but they have precious lessons to teach, and lessons that can be learned in no other school.

I am not preaching to you, my dear friend; and I should hardly venture to say all this, if I did not feel assured that your convictions, and your experience too, respond to such sentiments. You believe in the fatherly use of pain; you believe that when suffering comes to the children of God, God himself comes too, and often so fills the soul as to make one "rejoice in the Lord," however great the bodily anguish.

Nothing impresses me more than the heroism of the

hospital; the sublime triumph of Christian faith in chambers of suffering — suffering severe and sometimes prolonged. Distress itself is transfigured into joy in the Lord. Specimens may be found all about the Christian world. Miss Marsh, in her *English Hearts and Hands*, speaks of Henry Randall, one of the navvies she was wont to visit, who, as she entered the humble cottage, stretched out his emaciated hands, saying: "Oh, I am so happy! I wanted to see you to tell you I am so happy in Jesus Christ." Speaking of his brother, the Rev. John Cowper, William the poet says: "In a time of severe and continued suffering, he smiled in my face, and said: 'Brother, I am as happy as a king.'" Mrs. Ellis, wife of Dr. William Ellis, could say in the midst of her sufferings: "I think I have a foretaste of the heavenly world; it does not seem possible to enjoy more elevated delights than I experienced in the spiritual presence and love of my Saviour; I would rather continue on this bed of pain with my joy of mind, than be raised to any degree of health or earthly comfort, if, with it, I should have lukewarmness or coldness in love to God." In the Memoir of Dr. William Gordon, entitled, *The Christian Philosopher*, I remember the exclamation, "what joy I have had! no one can describe it! I have often told you, when in great pain, that I could not have conceived any human being could suffer so much. I am sure I may now say I could not conceive any human being could enjoy so much."

Testimonies such as these come from every condition of life, and from those to whom the most protracted visitation is allotted. Harriet Stoneman, who for seven and thirty years was "as gold tried in the fire," could say: "I experience so much of the Saviour's love in supporting me under pain, that I cannot fear its increase." And are not even the agonies of martyrdom sometimes drowned in a tide of holy joy? You will recall the two Augustinian monks, Henry and John, the first that were burnt in Germany, and John Rogers, first of bloody Mary's victims, who rejoiced in the midst of the flames; while Bainham protested: "In this fire I feel no more pain than if I were in a bed of down; it is to me as a bed of roses."

> " Spices crushed their fragrance yield ;
>   Trodden scents their sweets respire ;
> Would you have its strength revealed,
>   Cast the incense in the fire ;
> Thus the crushed and broken frame
>   Oft its sweetest graces yield ;
> And through suffering, toil and shame,
> From the martyr's keenest flame,
>   Heavenly incense is distilled."

XXX.

To My Friend Going Home,

A HAPPY NEW YEAR!

THE happiest of all your years — an hundred fold the happiest! So you look upon it as likely to prove. You hardly expect to be here at its close; you are looking forward to an entrance into our Father's house.

Your assurance of union to Him who is the resurrection and the life, and of ere long beholding his glory, gives great delight to me and to many another friend. In your room it seems but a very little way to heaven; and as for what lies between, it is not dying, but going home, going to where your chief treasures are laid up. It is not death that will remove you from earth, but the Lord Jesus, the conqueror of death and of him that hath the power of death. There is no last enemy to frown, but only the Saviour to smile upon you; and so you are now smiling upon him, and looking greatly pleased at the thought of seeing the door open soon to the marriage supper of the Lamb. You have no tears to shed over the announcement that this rough voyage is so nearly over, and that the haven is not far off. Knowing who is in the vessel, you have no fear of being shipwrecked into anything but the rest that remaineth for the people of God. Who can blame you for being a little homesick for heaven? Surely there is no place like home; and it sometimes requires a good deal of grace to be resigned to absence from that blessed abode.

"Almost well, and nearly at home," said Richard Baxter, worn by long labor and sickness. *Gute Nacht* — "Good night," said Neander, the church historian. This night of time was for him far spent; and falling asleep, he opened his eyes on the daybreak of eternity. I look upon you, my friend, with a sort of envy that you are certainly near perfect and perpetual health; near the end of annoyance from sin and infirmities; that you are no farther from the place for seeing the King in his beauty. If any one on earth should be cheerful and joyous, is it not the one who is waiting for the Master's home-call, which may come any day?

It was on a first of January that a precious little girl said to her friend; "You and I have spent many a New Year's Day together, but this will be the last. As a bird released from its cage, I shall fly away, and you cannot stop me." "It is New Year's Day," said the mother of Nathan Dickerman to her sick son. "Well, mamma," he replied, "I don't expect to see another New Year's here; but I expect I shall be where it is always New Year." Is it children only, in their simplicity and comparative ignorance, who talk thus? Many a Christian, ripe in the spiritual growth of years, uses similar language. "Dying is sweet work," said the Rev. Samuel Medley, "sweet work. I am looking up to my dear Jesus — my God, my portion, my all in all. Glory, Glory! Home, Heaven!"

> " To the saints while here below,
>   With New Years new mercies come ;
> But the happiest year they know
>   Is the last, which leads them home."